W9-CNB-637

INUNGUAK

THE LITTLE GREENLANDER

INUNGUAK
THE LITTLE GREENLANDER

BY PALLE PETERSEN

ILLUSTRATED BY JENS ROSING

LOTHROP, LEE & SHEPARD BOOKS
NEW YORK

N
W
E
S
GREENLAND
(KALAALIT NUNAAT)
GREENLAND SEA
BAFFIN BAY
BAFFIN ISLAND
Upernavik
Ittoqqortoormiit
Uummannaq
Qirqirtarsuaq
Ilulissat
Aasiaat
ICELAND
Sisimiut
Ammassalik
Maniitsoq
DAVIS STRAIT
STRAIT OF DENMARK
Nuuk
Paamiut
Narsaq
Qaqortoq
Nanortalik
NORTH AMERICA
NORTH ATLANTIC OCEAN

A NOTE FROM THE AUTHOR AND ILLUSTRATOR

The story of *Inunguak* takes place along the central western coast of *Kalaalit Nunaat*—"The Human Beings' Land," or Greenland. Greenland is the largest island in the world, but only a very narrow strip of its coastline is habitable, as 84 percent of the island's surface is covered by an age-old ice cap, in some places as deep as 10,000 feet. But Greenland's coastal waters teem with fish, whales, walrus, and seals, which at the time of this story provided the people with food, clothing, heat, and shelter.

The Greenlanders, who first came to the island about 5,000 years ago, called themselves *Inuit,* or "human beings," in contrast to spirits and the beings in the sea and sky. European explorers first came to Greenland in the 16th century. They were followed by hunters and fisherman, and in 1721 Greenland was Christianized. Today most native Greenlanders are of mixed European and Inuit descent.

In the area where *Inunguak* takes place, the months of May, June and July remain light around the clock, while October, November, December, and the first half of January are one long night, illuminated only by the Northern Lights, the stars, and the moon.

During the sunless months, a family might be trapped in the lodge for weeks by deadly snow storms and temperatures of −25° to −40° F. At the time this story takes place, winter was spent at indoor tasks and listening to the elders, especially the grandmothers, tell stories. Summer was a time for hunting, fishing, and preparing meat and hides for the coming winter.

The Inuit always shared what there was to eat, but given their harsh climate and living conditions, there wasn't always enough to go around. The old, the weak, and the inept often chose death in the sea or ice over becoming a burden on the others. This may seem cruel to people who live in gentler climates, but the Inuit believed that death was as great a gift as life. A boy like Inunguak caused his father concern, for fear he would not be able to hunt and thus to live.

The Inuit honored and believed in *Norrivik,* "The Mother of the Sea," a spirit who, as her hair was combed, sent whales and seals for them to catch. In a trance, the *angakkoq* (shaman) could honor and serve her, and even comb her hair, just as he could fend off evil spirits.

Although the Inuit of Greenland share some traditions with many of their North American arctic cousins, their way of life, molded by their harsh climate and isolation, was and still is unique.

Many years ago, in a little village in Greenland, there lived a great hunter. He caught many seals and whales and even polar bears. There were always furs and plenty of food in his longhouse. His wife was a skillful seamstress and made the warmest *kamiks* in the village. The only thing they lacked was a child, but the seasons came and went and no child was born.

Then came the hardest winter anyone could remember. The cold was so bitter that the men could rarely go out to hunt. And that winter the woman at last gave birth to a child.

"Inuk," she whispered when she looked at the little one, the Greenlander word for Man. But the baby was very small, so his father called him *Inunguak*—Little Man.

Afraid that he would not survive to see the spring, his mother carried the baby next to her body, keeping him warm beneath her sealskin coat, and Inunguak lived through that hard winter. During the summer he grew stronger, and by the following winter he could toddle about.

Several other families lived in the same longhouse, and there were always other children for Inunguak to play with. But though the other boys practiced throwing harpoons and making tools like the grown men, Inunguak preferred to sit with his grandfather.

Grandfather had once been a strong hunter and a fine storyteller. Now he was too old to hunt and his voice was weak. No one wanted to listen to the old man anymore. Still, he continued to tell the old stories and legends of the People. When he spoke, the words, though hushed, came alive in his mouth, and Inunguak soaked up all the old tales, even when he did not truly understand them.

"Inunguak will never become a great hunter," said the people of the village. "All he does is listen to stories, and stories are useless."

Yet night after night by the light of the blubber lamp, Inunguak listened to Grandfather.

"I am not really the storyteller," Grandfather told Inunguak. "Our ancestors are speaking though me. These stories came to me from my father and my grandfather; they may be as old as humankind. I was a child like you when I heard the story about the first Inuit—the first People."

Once, there was only sky. But a long, long time ago, there was a great rockslide in the sky. Mountains and dirt came tumbling down, and that is how the Earth came into being.

Then the first People grew out of the Earth. Little children sprang up between the low willow bushes and were fed by the Earth. One pair of them grew big and became Man and Woman. The man went hunting and brought back meat for the children. The woman made clothes and a home for the little ones so they could survive through the winter, and the children lived and grew and became the People. That is why this country is called ***Inuit Nunat****, the Land of the People.*

During the day, Inunguak's father took the boy with him in his kayak to teach him to hunt. He showed his son the secrets of the animals. He taught him where the birds hide among the ice mountains and where the seals have their breathing holes.

"Someday you will be a great hunter," he said, and he made Inunguak a small harpoon to use. But Inunguak could not hit his target.

The other boys came home proud of their large catches. They teased Inunguak because he always missed.

Finally Inunguak's father took him to the village shaman, a wise man who dealt with the spirit world. "Can you find any spirits to help my boy?" he asked.

The shaman looked at Inunguak for a long time. At last he spoke: "This child has good spirits in him. Someday he will be a great man." Then the shaman gave Inunguak the foot of a snowy owl. "This amulet will protect you," he said, and Inunguak wore it always.

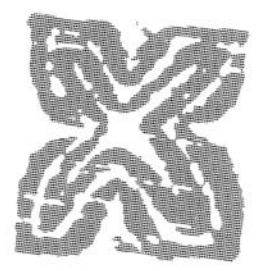

In the long Greenland winter, the sun is gone for many weeks, and it is hard to go hunting. The Greenlanders use dogs and sleds to go far out on the ice to the good hunting places. Grandfather told Inunguak how the People got dogs:

The number of men grew and they wanted animals to pull them. One man stamped on the ground and shouted, "Hoc, hoc hoc!" Then dogs leaped out of little tufts of grass. They had puppies, and so there were more dogs. The men hitched them to sleds so they could ride over the land and far out on the ice.

Inunguak's father tried to teach him to drive the dogsled, but the dogs would not obey the boy's calls. They ran wherever they pleased, no matter how much Inunguak shouted. The other boys made fun of him because a boy has to be able to control his dogs.

Finally Inunguak's father gave up on making him a hunter.

"Let him stay with his grandfather," advised the shaman. "Perhaps one day the old stories can be put to some use."

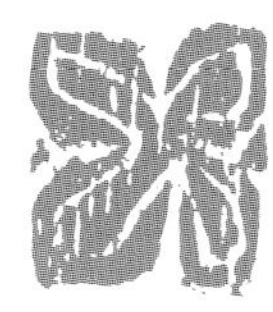

The villagers were like one big family. The Greenlanders shared their catch in bad times so no one went hungry. But they often forgot to give food to Inunguak and his grandfather. And when they remembered, Inunguak often forgot to eat it.

"They must hunt, too," said the other hunters. "One cannot live on stories."

Inunguak became pale and thin. Day after day he sat with his ear close to the old man's mouth so that he could hear.

"Inunguak is as weak as a girl," the other boys teased.

"You must eat," whispered Grandfather. "Meat will make you strong." And Grandfather told this story:

Once upon a time, the People did not know the sun. They had to live in the dark. One day, the sun suddenly rose. They could see how beautiful the Earth was. They went out hunting to get good meat to eat. That is how the Inuit grew great and strong.

Then Inunguak began to eat more often.

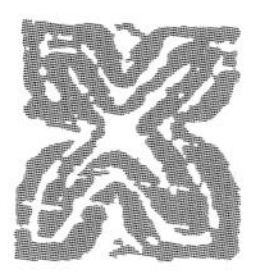

One summer day, strange ships came to the village. They were as big as icebergs.

The Greenlanders stared at the weird beings who rowed ashore in small boats. "They are as white as dirty snow," said the villagers. "They are ugly and have no color. They speak like dogs. Can these be real people?"

The foreigners wanted to trade strange things that no one had seen before: glass beads, colored cloth, mirrors, and sharp knives made of iron. In return they wanted good furs, blubber, and walrus tusks.

Grandfather grew worried. "I must see these foreigners," he whispered. "Inunguak, let me lean on you."

Grandfather had not left the house for many summers. The bright light blinded him, but he had to warn the People. "You must not trade with these strangers," he whispered. "They bring misfortune."

The shaman mistrusted the foreigners, too. He tried to drive them away by chanting his songs and beating his drum. But when they heard the noise, the strangers just shivered with laughter, as if they were dogs.

"You must not give away good fur and blubber," whispered Grandfather. "These strangers are not Inuit, they are not real People. They are *kavdlunaks* like in the story."

In the old days, in a small village, there lived a man and his wife. They had a daughter who could not hold on to any man. "You should have a dog for a husband," said her father.

Sometime later, a big dog came and dragged the girl out of the house. The dog and the girl had children, but the children were greedy and ate all the seals their grandfather could catch. One day they even ate the grandfather.

Their mother was very angry at them. She took a boot sole from a ***kamik****, put her children in the sole, and pushed it out to sea. "Now take care of yourselves," she shouted after them.*

The children of the girl and the dog are called ***kavdlunaks****. Whenever they return they bring misfortune with them.*

But the villagers did not listen to Grandfather's story. They traded away their best furs and blubber for sharp knives and bright cloth.

With the first snowfall, the *kavdlunaks* disappeared. Winter hit hard and cold. There were not enough warm skins and dried meat in the village. The People froze and starved. Many died, including Inunguak's own father and mother.

The old ones lay down to die in order to spare food for the young. "Death is a joy for old people, Inunguak," said Grandfather. "Now listen to my final story."

Once upon a time, the Earth was dark and there was no joy for the People. They did not know death.

One day two old women were talking. "We can do without light," said one of them, "as long as we are without death." She was afraid of death.

"No," answered the other. "We want both light and death."

And so it was. Light and death came to the Earth. One of the women died. They covered her up with a pile of stones, so she could no longer walk. Even so, she came back and poked her head out from beneath the bed.

The other woman pushed the dead one back. "We are going out hunting and we cannot take you with us on our sled," she said. The dead one had to stay where she was when the living people left.

Then Grandfather died. They buried him under a pile of stones.

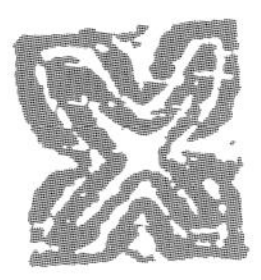

The shaman called the survivors together in his house. "I will chase away the evil spirits that the *kavdlunaks* brought with them," he said.

The blubber lamp flickered and cast shadows about the room. The shaman sat down on a skin in the middle of the floor and put his drum in front of him. "Inunguak!" he called. "Bind my hands!"

The boy tied the shaman's hands behind his back.

Suddenly the spirits blew out the lamp. Everything vanished in the dark.

"Goi, goi, goi!" cried a voice. There was beating on the drum and rattling and roaring in the house.

The evil spirits came out of the dark. The shaman fought with them, and the spirits squealed and howled and laughed and cried while the drumbeat pounded on.

Then all was still. Fear crept into the house like a huge black-armed beast that screeched with anger and stomped over the beds.

"Inunguak!" it shouted. Everyone fled into the corners. "Inunguak!"

The boy stood up. He lit the lamp.

Howling with rage, the monster disappeared into the darkness.

So the evil spirits were driven away from the village, but the shaman lay senseless on the floor. Everyone stared at Inunguak. "Look!" they said. "He is no longer a Little Man; he has become an *Inuk*, a real Man."

"What now, Inunguak?" they asked. "Where are the animals that will feed us? Where is the good hunting?"

Inunguak remembered one of Grandfather's stories. "Do you know the story of the Mother of the Sea?" he asked.

No—the People had forgotten about her. "We need food now more than stories," they said.

"The stories can help us," Inunguak told them. "We must go to the Mother of the Sea. She will send her animals to us."

The cold was still bitter. Most of the People were too weak or afraid to go out onto the dark ice.

Inunguak hitched the last dogs in the village to his father's sled. They were so exhausted from hunger that they obeyed his smallest shout. He took his father's harpoon and ran behind the sled, across the ice, following the moon.

"Mother of the Sea, help us!" he cried.

Underneath the thick ice, deep down in the ocean, sat the Mother of the Sea. She laughed at the little man who dared to go out to the desolate sea to find food for his village.

Seals, walruses, whales—all the animals of the sea sat as close as lice in her long hair. She shook her head and combed them free. Up they swam, up to the boy on the ice.

Suddenly Inunguak saw a vast crack in the ice. It boiled with warmth and life. The animals of the sea had come to the crack to breathe.

Inunguak lifted his harpoon. It was as if the animals offered themselves to him. "Take us, Inunguak," they seemed to say. "We want to give new strength to the People."

Inunguak took as many as he could load on his sled. He gave some meat to the dogs to give them strength to pull homeward as hard as they could.

When they heard the dogs, the People came crawling out of their houses. "It is Inunguak!" they cried. "He has come with food from the Mother of the Sea!"

Inunguak cut up a large seal and gave out the meat. At last, the People could eat until they were full, and there was still enough for the rest of the winter.

"The hunter is great, but the storyteller is greater," said the People as they filled their shrunken bellies. "In the story it is told how it all starts, and a story can be told over and over again."

Then they feasted in the little village in Greenland, and the People could laugh and sing once more. "Aja, ajajaja." The shaman beat on his drum. And Inunguak said, "Listen to this story. . . ."

Once, there was only the sky. . .

Printed in the United States of America

First U.S. edition 1993. 1 2 3 4 5 6 7 8 9 10

Library of Congress Cataloging in Publication Data
Petersen, Palle, [Inunguak, den lille grønlænder. English] Inunguak, the little Greenlander / by Palle Petersen ; illustrated by Jens Rosing. p. cm. Translation of : Inunguak, den lille grønlænder. Summary: The other Inuit boys ridicule little Inunguak, who cannot hunt and spends all his time listening to his grandfather's old stories of the People, until bad times come to Greenland and the stories become useful. ISBN 0-688-09876-2.—ISBN 0-688-09877-0 (lib. bdg.) 1. Eskimos—Greenland—Juvenile fiction. [1. Eskimos—Greenland—Fiction. 2. Indians—Greenland—Fiction. 3. Greenland—Fiction.] I. Rosing, Jens, ill. II. Title. PZ7.P44198In 1990 [Fic]—dc20 90-40472 CIP AC